The HOUNDS of
PENHALLOW HALL

THE HIDDEN STAIRCASE

For William
HW

~

STRIPES PUBLISHING
An imprint of the Little Tiger Group
1 Coda Studios
189 Munster Road,
London SW6 6AW

A paperback original
First published in Great Britain in 2018

Text copyright © Holly Webb, 2018
Illustrations copyright © Jason Cockcroft, 2018

Author photograph copyright © Nigel Bird

ISBN: 978-1-84715-915-1

The right of Holly Webb and Jason Cockcroft to be identified
as the author and illustrator of this work respectively has been asserted by them
in accordance with the Copyright, Designs and Patents Act, 1988.

Printed and bound in the UK.

2 4 6 8 10 9 7 5 3 1

The HOUNDS of PENHALLOW HALL

THE HIDDEN STAIRCASE

Stripes

I

Last Day of the Holidays

"You might even enjoy school," Rex whispered, and Polly wriggled as his wiry muzzle tickled her ear. "Having some real children to talk to, instead of dogs and ghosts."

"Oi," William muttered, rolling over to peer into the murky water.

Magnus lifted his great head from his paws for a moment and gave a dismissive snort, as if to say that he was better company than any *child*.

"I *like* talking to you." Polly sighed. William had been born over a hundred years before she had but even though he was a ghost, he was chatty and fun – when he decided to turn up. She knew it would seem bizarre to anyone else, but the ghost of William, a little boy who had once lived at Penhallow Hall, and the dog spirits that inhabited the statues there, had become Polly's closest friends since she and her mother had arrived. "I know it won't be so bad in a couple of weeks, when I'm not new any more. But I've still got to get through my first day."

Polly shuddered and grabbed another huge handful of waterweed. She was trying to clear the tiny stream in the old Chinese garden so that the water would run properly through the lily pond.

Polly loved the Chinese garden, with its rickety old pagoda and the clumps of whispering bamboo. She had first found it a few weeks before, when she had met the little

Pekingese who lived in a porcelain statue on the mantelpiece in the Red Drawing Room. Li-Mei loved the Chinese garden, too – it reminded her of her beloved owner, Sarah. It would be amazing to see the garden all cleaned up and perfect again, and Stephen the Head Gardener had been delighted when Polly suggested tidying it up a bit. Eventually he wanted all of the gardens at Penhallow to be open for visitors. For now, though, she was glad that it was just her and William and the dogs. It was so peaceful.

"School is very important," Rex pronounced grandly, and Polly turned round to glare into his dark eyes.

"You don't know!" she pointed out. "You've never been to school, Rex."

"I liked school," William put in. "Most of the time. Except I couldn't take Magnus with me."

He stretched out on the bank, looking up at the sky. "The day I came back from school, I always used to go exploring with Magnus all round Penhallow – the gardens, the wood, everything. It was as if I had to see it all, to make sure it was real…"

Polly nodded. At least she would be able to come home from school every afternoon. When he was even younger than her, William had been sent away to boarding school. Polly had read books about schools like that, but she couldn't imagine going to one for real. Not even midnight feasts would make up for being away from home for so long.

Polly laid down her handful of weeds and

wiped her grubby hands on her shorts. Then she sat down next to Rex for a rest.

Home. Penhallow was home now. She'd only been here since the start of the summer holidays but it already felt as though she belonged. She loved the ancient house and she loved its dogs even more.

At Penhallow, the dogs never left. They slept in statues, in paintings, even in the carvings on the old wooden banisters. She had first woken Rex soon after she'd moved in and she knew that there were so many more dogs hidden in the house, so many more stories to find out. She wandered around the rooms sometimes, looking at the dogs peering back at her from the portraits and wondering which of them would be the next to wake.

Perhaps Rex and the others were right, and school wouldn't be so bad. It wasn't as if she'd liked her old school very much. It had been fine before her dad died but afterwards everything had changed. It felt as though everyone was tiptoeing around her, fussing over her, whispering about her. Polly had hated it, even though deep down she knew that her friends and the teachers were just trying to help.

"Do you think I'll have to say anything about my dad?" she whispered, and William and Magnus leaned closer to hear. Polly had assumed that being actually dead would mean that ghosts were quite good at understanding how people felt when they were grieving, but it didn't seem to work that way.

"Er. Do you want to?" William asked uncomfortably and Magnus laid his ears back.

"No!"

William shrugged. "Can't you just not mention it then?"

Polly rolled her eyes. "What if someone asks me?"

"Um. Thump them?"

Polly turned to stare at him. "Is that what you'd do?"

"Probably. I might tell them to shut up first and only thump them if they didn't."

"I thought your school was really expensive and smart?" Polly said. "If I hit somebody I'd probably get expelled. *And* they'd hit me back. What good would that do?"

"It might make you feel better. I don't know! I'm only trying to help."

Polly took a deep breath. "Sorry," she murmured. "I'm just … panicking."

William sighed. "All right. So maybe don't thump them. I'm not sure that anyone will ask. And if they do, can't you just say that you don't have a father?"

Polly swallowed hard and hunched her shoulders. "I do have one," she whispered. "He's just not here any more."

Rex moved closer to her, pressing against her back and resting his chin on her shoulder so that she was wrapped in his golden-grey fur. His warm breath huffed against her cheek and she turned to put her arms round him. She had hugged him often but she had never felt so clearly that he was hugging her back.

"I didn't mean that to sound the way it did," William muttered. Magnus was glaring at him, Polly saw as she glanced up. It looked as if the great grey wolfhound had just barged the ghost-boy with his muzzle, shoving him on to his feet to apologize. Which was odd, because Magnus would normally leap to his boy's defence.

"I know," Polly told William. "I suppose I'll just try not to mention it." She heaved a huge sigh. "Oh well. Wish me luck…"

William snorted. "It's the rest of your form that needs it, not you."

Polly rolled her eyes. "I know you're a ghost but I bet I could still shove you in the lily pond."

"So, everyone, this is Polly." Miss Roberts smiled down at her and Polly looked at somewhere slightly above her feet.

"Polly's come from a school in London," the teacher went on. "That's right, isn't it?"

"Yes…"

"And I expect that was quite a lot larger than we are here? This is a mixed Year Five and Year Six class. Did Mrs Jones explain that?"

Polly nodded. She and her mum had had a sort of interview with the head teacher the week before. She'd explained that the school was too small to have separate classes for each year group.

"I'm sure you'll get used to it very quickly," Miss Roberts said, patting Polly's shoulder. "Now, I think we'll put you here. Lucy and Martha will look after you, won't you, girls?" She steered Polly towards an empty chair and Polly dropped into it gratefully. It seemed odd to have plastic-topped tables and an electronic whiteboard, just like at her old school, when the building itself looked so old.

"Hi," the girl next to her whispered, and the one across the table added, "Hi, Polly."

Her voice seemed vaguely familiar and Polly glanced up. It was the girl she had met when she'd gone with Mum to buy her school uniform, the red sweatshirt that she was wearing now. That was Lucy, then – she remembered the girl's mum calling her name.

So the one next to Polly with the sleek whitish fair hair had to be Martha. She was smiling eagerly at Polly and she looked quite friendly. Polly's heart stopped thumping quite so hard and she managed a small smile back.

Polly made an effort to look over at Lucy and smile, but Lucy hardly glanced up at all. Polly remembered that she'd seemed chatty when they'd met at the uniform shop.

Polly tried to listen as Miss Roberts explained about their topic for the term, and the mum who'd be coming in to teach them French, and which days PE would be, but it all seemed to be floating over her head. She stared down at the pile of exercise books she'd been given and wondered whether she could get away without saying anything for the rest of the day.

Lucy and Martha scooped her up as the bell rang for the mid-morning break, and Miss

Roberts nodded approvingly as they swept her outside with them.

"Show Polly where everything is, please, you two!" she called after them.

Polly found herself out in the playground, sitting on the flat wooden edge of the little ones' sandpit, with most of the girls in her class gathered round and staring at her curiously.

"So why've you moved here, then?" Martha demanded.

"I told you!" Lucy leaned over from Polly's other side. "Her mum works at Penhallow Hall."

"Oh, yeah." Martha waved dismissively. "You live there, too?"

Polly nodded. "In a flat up on the top floor."

"Must be weird with all those visitors."

You don't know the half of it, Polly thought, trying not to smile. "It is a bit," she agreed. "It's nice when they all go home though." She tried to think of something to ask back. "Um, so have all of you always lived here?" she said, looking around at the little group of girls.

Most of the girls nodded but one of them said, "Just for two years. My parents came down here to set up a sailing school."

"Anna's the only new girl our year's had since

Reception," Lucy told Polly. "Until you. Loads of people come to Penhallow for holidays but not many move here to live."

"Oh." Polly nodded. That did sort of explain why they were all staring at her. "Er, so … what's Miss Roberts like? Is she nice?"

"She's all right. She's a bit strict sometimes." Martha made a face. "And she's got this thing about topic work – she goes way over the top. You know she said it was the Second World War this term? Just you wait, we'll be dressing up, I bet you."

"Building bomb shelters out of papier mâché," one of the other girls put in gloomily.

"Writing poems about air raids. She just has to make everything fit in… Even the maths. It'll be about how many bombs fell on Tuesday if it was a quarter as many as the day before. Or something."

Polly nodded. "We were doing Egypt last year. There was a lot of counting the stones in pyramids."

And building Egyptian sarcophagi, she remembered, half closing her eyes. She had been in a group with three of her friends. But she'd hardly spoken to them for weeks, too upset to talk, and they hadn't known how to talk to her. She had worked on her own little part of the coffin in silence, hating the way that her teacher dropped her voice to a whisper every time she mentioned death or dying in front of Polly. After the first couple of afternoons she'd told her mum she felt sick and for once Mum had believed her. Polly had spent the rest of the week lying on the sofa, with Gran fussing around and making her soup.

Martha nodded. "Yeah, we did Egypt, too."

She looked over her shoulder at Lucy and the other girl ducked her head as though she didn't want to meet Martha's eyes.

Polly glanced between them uncertainly – what did that odd look mean? Something seemed to be going on between the two of them.

"Leave me alone," Lucy said, so quietly that Polly was sure she was the only one who heard.

"Everything all right, girls?" Miss Roberts said as she came walking past them. "Are you finding your way around OK, Polly?"

Polly nodded, and then added in a rush, "Actually, Lucy was going to show me the library." Lucy hadn't said she would but Polly felt sure that she would agree – she looked as though she was desperate to get away.

"Oh, yes, good idea. It's quite new – the

parents raised a lot of money to get all those beanbags. We're very proud of it, aren't we? You take Polly and show her, Lucy." Miss Roberts stood there smiling and watching as they went back inside. Martha was watching them, too, arms folded and scowling.

"Thanks," Lucy mumbled, as they disappeared in the door. And then, "There. Library. OK?" At that she turned tail and hurried away, leaving Polly in the doorway staring after her.

Polly's mum met her as she came back to the house, eager to hear about her first day. She'd even nipped out and got Polly a present – a new top with birds embroidered on it.

"I knew how worried you were about school," she'd said as Polly hugged her thank you. "I'm so proud of you. It *was* all right, wasn't it, Poll? You're not just saying it to make me feel better?"

"It was OK," Polly promised. And it sort of had been, depending on how she looked at it. Everyone had been helpful and no one had asked about her dad. The work hadn't been hard – it was odd being in a mixed-age group but Polly was sure she'd get used to it. "And it was sort of nice, walking back on my own."

"You're so grown up." Her mum stroked her hair. "Here, look. I went to the baker's as well and got you a flapjack as a treat. That'll keep you going till dinner."

Polly headed outside to the gardens, pulling her flapjack out of its bag once she was away from the precious furniture inside the house. She knew exactly where she was going – to the terrace, to Rex. She sat down on the steps to talk to the two dogs, lying above her on their pedestals, but there were too many people around for them to talk back. It was a gorgeous sunny afternoon and lots of visitors were wandering about, admiring the late summer flowers.

"It was better than I thought it would be," she told Rex slowly. "I mean, I was expecting it to be strange but actually everyone in the class was really friendly. Well, except Lucy… You know, the girl I met at the uniform shop. She was being a bit weird…" Polly looked up at Rex's noble stone face. She wasn't even sure if he was listening but it was still so comforting to talk to him. She let out a little sigh and leaned back against the warm stone.

Perhaps – just perhaps – everything was going to be OK?

2

The Dog in the Nursery

Each day that week, Polly came back home after school and sat on the steps, leaning lovingly against her stone dog.

It was getting better – slowly. At least she knew where everything was now and she knew the names of most of the people in her class. It helped that the school was tiny. But it was hard work, being back at school every single day. Polly had spent the long summer holiday exploring Penhallow, while Mum had been busy settling into her new job. She could get up when she liked (mostly) and grab her own breakfast halfway through the morning. That helped when she'd been out in the middle of the night, exploring the moonlit beach with Rex. Now she was up at seven and back wearing school uniform instead of comfy jeans.

She rested her back against Rex's pedestal and dozed.

"She's not going to make it, just look at her. It's only Wednesday."

Polly opened one eye a slit and glared at William. "Go away. I was sleeping."

"It's not even as if you had to roll around in the mud playing rugby," he said. "Or get up at six to go for a run before breakfast."

Polly opened the other eye. "Is that what you had to do? That does actually make me feel better."

"Happy to help."

Magnus snorted and then licked her ear. Polly peered round at him in surprise – Magnus was hardly ever affectionate to her. Both dogs had been solid stone on their pedestals when she'd arrived back from school. The gardens must be empty now if the dogs had shaken off their stone forms. How long had she slept for?

"Mum'll be wondering where I am," she murmured sleepily.

"She knows." Rex tugged at the fleece top that was draped round Polly's shoulders. "Look."

"Oh!" It was her mum's dark blue Penhallow fleece. "She put it round me?"

"Mm-hm. She spotted you and laughed to herself, and then I heard her murmur that it was getting chilly." He nudged her cheek with his wiry muzzle. "What's wrong, Polly? Why are you so tired?"

Polly sighed. "It's just … tricky. Getting to know what everybody's like, when they've all known each other for years and years. And the two girls I have to sit with, they've got some sort of fight going on. Half the time they're snapping at each other and the other half it's like they're best friends again. I'm not sure about Martha but I really like Lucy. She's mad about animals – she's got animal key rings all over her backpack, bunches and bunches of them."

"Perhaps you need something to take your mind off all that," William suggested, leaning over to look at her. "We could find another of the dogs. A story, that's what you need."

Polly glanced up, blinking away her sleepiness. "Maybe…" She half wanted to but she wasn't sure. Perhaps William was right though – the story of another of the Penhallow dogs would take her mind off school.

"There's that dog up in the nursery." Magnus walked down the steps and came to sit in front of her and William. "That threadbare old thing on the shelf near the doll's house. He reminds me of her." He leaned forwards to sniff at Polly and then sat back, looking almost triumphant. "Lonely," he pronounced. "Yes, just the same."

"I'm not lonely," Polly protested. "I'm fine!"

"Mmmm." Rex looked at her thoughtfully and then gave his ears a brisk shake. "No. She needs cheering up, Magnus, you old fool. We don't want a sad story making her feel worse." He pushed Polly gently, just under her elbow, to make her stand. "Go on upstairs, Polly. Your mother will be coming back to find you any minute." He licked her hand. "And stop worrying…"

Polly meant to do as Rex said – to go upstairs and thank Mum for wrapping her up in the fleece. But somehow, when she should have turned towards the tower staircase, she found that she was making for the nursery corridor instead. She had been there lots of times – it was where William had grown up and where she had first met his ghost. She would have thought that she knew all the toys scattered about the room but she couldn't remember the old toy dog that Magnus had talked about.

As she walked along the passageway she could feel the house moving and breathing around her. Not just the tiny specks of dust dancing in the light of the evening sun, or the footfalls of the staff tidying up for the night, but something in the house itself. Polly wasn't really sure what it was but she knew her mum felt it, too, a bit. She'd watched Mum walk up the main stairs and gently stroke her hand across the little wooden beasts in the carved banisters. Stephen was the same with the way he spoke about the gardens.

Polly knew that Rex was part of it, and that the way she loved him bound her to the house and the story of Penhallow. It made her feel as though she truly belonged. After trying so hard to fit in at her new school all day, walking through the passages and breathing in the faint scent of dust and furniture polish and scones was like wrapping herself in a blanket.

So when she went into the nursery, the sense of loss and loneliness was all the more of a shock. The dog's unhappiness seemed to well up around her so that she almost staggered back against the doorframe.

Go away.

Polly stood there, blinking. She had felt something like this before, when she and Rex had first gone to talk to William – a sense that he was miserable and just wanted to be left alone. But this was so much stronger.

Polly gazed up at the shelf by the doll's house, clenching her fists so tightly that her nails dug in. *I'm not going*, she said firmly in her head. She didn't know if the dog could hear her but even if he couldn't, saying it made her feel more determined.

The toy dog lay slumped on the shelf, completely still. He was a greyish white, and Polly thought that once he would have been soft and furry, but now the fur was worn away in patches and one of his glass eyes was missing. He looked terribly sad, even without Polly knowing his story.

"You look like you're a hundred miles away."

Polly blinked and realized that one of the volunteers was standing next to her.

"Lizzie, why is that toy dog up there? I mean, is it a special one?"

Lizzie looked where she was pointing and smiled. "Oh, I love him. I'm so glad he's on show – he's not valuable, I suppose, but he is special. They found him in an old trunk, with a little note explaining whose he was. He belonged to one of the children who was evacuated to Penhallow during the Second World War. There were two elderly sisters living here then – it was after the family had left, of course. Quite a lot of the house was shut up because it was hard to get staff during the war, but the sisters lived in part of it. Mrs Ford and Miss Laleham, they were called. They took in evacuees from London. I imagine the little girl must have left him behind. Mrs Ford had put a label on him but it fell apart – it was very fragile."

"Oh…" Polly whispered. "I wonder why he got left. Thank you for telling me." She turned away, biting her lip. Perhaps Rex was right – the story was just too sad.

Despite her tiredness the night before, Polly woke early the next morning. There was a heavy, warm weight next to her, and Rex lifted his head and gazed at her sleepily.

"You slept on my feet!" Polly stroked his ears lovingly. Perhaps that was why she felt so happy.

Rex nuzzled her ear. "Better go. Need to be back in the gardens for opening time. I can't slope off too often or people might start to notice the statue's gone. Enjoy school today. You will, I promise." He blew into her ear and Polly nodded, wondering if he'd given her a little of his magic.

She hopped out of bed and pulled on her school uniform. After breakfast she set off through the grounds to school, nipping round to the terrace first to rub Rex's ears.

"Hi, Polly!"

Polly jumped sideways as Stephen peered out at her from behind the branches of a climbing rose. He hopped down off the ladder, smiling at her apologetically. "Sorry! I didn't mean to scare you. I was just mending the trellis. Are you all right? I thought you'd seen me or I wouldn't have shouted like that."

"I'm OK – I wasn't paying attention, that's all. I'm fine." Polly smiled at him.

"Right... Oh, by the way, if you see a dog around, can you let me know?"

"A dog?" Polly froze, her smile fading. Had Stephen seen Rex? Or Magnus, or Li-Mei? When Polly had first met Rex, she'd worried about her mum and other people in the house seeing him but it seemed that not many people did. The occasional visitor would blink as Rex went past, as though they'd seen the tip of a tail disappearing round a corner. Polly could only see Rex because he chose to let her, Polly had realized over the summer. But did that mean that Stephen knew the secret, too?

"What sort of dog?" she asked, trying not to sound panicked.

"Oh. Scruffy little grey thing with a floppy ear. Friendly looking, quite young, I should think. I'm just wondering if he's a stray.

There didn't seem to be anyone with him and I didn't notice a collar. He was wandering across the South Lawn, over towards the village path. As you're going that way for school, can you keep an eye out?"

Polly nodded. "Definitely." That didn't sound like Rex or any of the other dogs she knew – so perhaps it really was a stray? Or another Penhallow dog had woken without them knowing. "I'll let you know if I spot him. See you later!"

She hurried along the path and out across the South Lawn, making for the folly – the little stone building that looked like a Roman temple. Just beyond it there was a gate that led out to the cliff path – Polly's favourite way to walk into the village and to school. Later in the year, when it was really cold and windy, she might go along the road instead, but for now she loved the little path. It was so narrow and twisty that Polly reckoned it had been made by rabbits, not people. She saw them occasionally – little sandy brown rabbits that hopped out from under her feet and darted away into the tangle of brambles and gorse.

Polly scurried into the playground just as the bell was going, too late to chat to anyone. It was a relief, actually, not having to smile and try to join in. Maybe she should be late every day, she thought to herself as she hung her jacket in the cloakroom.

Lucy smiled at her as she sat down and Polly smiled back without even thinking about it.

"That was close," she whispered to Lucy. "I must have taken ages eating breakfast or something."

Lucy nodded. "My gran has this thing about breakfast being the most important meal of the day. She makes loads and she looks really sad if I don't eat everything. I can't break it to her that I hate porridge."

Polly could feel Martha on the other side of Lucy, sucking in a breath to say something sarcastic. She jumped in, babbling, "Me, too! It's so sticky – like eating glue."

Lucy shot her a grateful look and then nudged her in the ribs – Miss Roberts was eyeing them as though she strongly suspected they hadn't been listening.

"I'd like you to work in pairs for this, please. That might mean a bit of moving around – just for our topic work, so no complaining! And no, before you ask, you can't choose your own partners, I have a list." Miss Roberts searched her desk for a moment and then held it up triumphantly. "Here we are."

She went on to read out the pairs, mostly one boy, one girl. Polly listened anxiously, hoping her partner would be somebody she'd at least spoken to before. "Polly, I've put you with Lucy. I thought that would be easier as she's already been showing you around."

"What about me?" Martha asked indignantly. "I'm showing her around, too."

"Yes, but I want pairs, not threes. You're with Kieran, Martha, so you can go and sit at that table by the bookcase, please."

Martha shot Lucy a look and grabbed her pencil case to stomp across the room. Lucy and Polly looked at each other, relieved, and suddenly Polly decided to stop being cautious. Why shouldn't she just ask?

"Why is Martha being mean to you?" she said, keeping her voice low. "You've all been friends since you started school. She hasn't always been like this, has she?"

Lucy stared down at the table and shook her head. "No," she said. "Only since last year." She looked up at Polly, peering through the wavy blond hair that she'd let fall over her face. "We used to do loads of stuff together but now… Well, we don't. We're just different. We always used to mess about in class. Martha's good at that – she made me laugh all the time. But I suppose I grew out of it. You know we were talking about that topic we did last year on Egypt? We found out so much stuff, and it was weird and bits of it were gory, and I loved it. My dad even took me to London to go and see all these mummies in a museum."

She glanced quickly up at Polly and then looked down, fiddling with the zip on her pencil case. "My mum and dad split up around then – and that didn't help me get on with Martha either. I suppose I wasn't the nicest person to be around. My dad's living in London now. I don't get to see him very much."

Lucy groaned, looking down at the pencil case – the zip tab had broken off in her hand. "I've only just got this. Mum's going to be cross. And all my stuff's in it!"

"Don't worry. Look, it's only the tab." Polly pulled a paper clip out of her own pencil case, feeling grateful that Mum had bought her every possible bit of stationery she could ever want. "Here." She looped the paper clip through the hole. "It doesn't look as nice, but at least it'll work." She pushed it back to Lucy and murmured, "You know, I haven't got a dad either."

Lucy's eyes widened. "Your parents split up, too? When? Was it a long time ago?"

"January. But they didn't split. My dad died." Lucy was only the second person she'd told, Polly realized. The first had been Rex.

"Sorry," Lucy muttered, and Polly scowled at her.

"Don't! Don't start thinking you have to tiptoe around me like anything you say's going to make me start crying. That's what happened at my old school and I hated it. I was glad to come here and leave it behind. I wasn't going to tell anybody about my dad so they couldn't make that face."

"OK…" Lucy nodded, and Polly could see her trying to twist her mouth into a smile.

"Don't do that, the wind might change and it'll stick." It was what Polly's gran said whenever she pulled a face.

Lucy gave a little snort of laughter and Polly grinned. Then she noticed the cute white dog on Lucy's pencil case and said, "Hey, have you seen…" She was about to ask Lucy about the stray dog that Stephen had mentioned, but Miss Roberts was eyeing them as she passed their table.

"Follow me at break," Lucy whispered to Polly as Miss Roberts started a video on the whiteboard. "Before Martha can catch up with us, all right? Tell me then."

As the bell rang, Lucy pulled Polly out of her seat and hurried her across the playground to an enormous chestnut tree, so wide that sitting behind the trunk they were hidden from everyone else.

"What were you going to ask me?" Lucy said curiously.

"Oh – the gardener up at the hall said he saw a stray dog. Yesterday, I think. A little white one. I just thought you might know if anybody in the village had lost their dog."

Lucy shook her head. "No one's said anything. I bet my gran would have told me – she gets all the gossip when she goes to the shops. And I haven't seen any posters up."

Then she frowned. "You know, I *did* see a white dog yesterday, too. Walking down the lane close by our cottage. Do you think it was the same one?"

"It sounds like it." Polly nodded.

"Poor dog…" Lucy looked worried. "I just thought he was a bit ahead of his owner, I didn't think he was all on his own." She gave a tiny sigh. "I hope he's OK." She glanced sideways at Polly. "I love dogs."

"Me, too," Polly agreed, wishing she could tell her the secret of Penhallow's dogs. Lucy would love Rex so much…

3

An Unhappy Ghost

The following afternoon, Rex met Polly halfway along the clifftop path, jumping and sniffing around her like a puppy, and she kneeled to hug him. He was taller than her when he stood on his hind paws and very heavy, so it was safer that way.

"I've missed you," he mumbled, as he licked her ears.

"I've missed you, too," Polly said. "But at least we've got the weekend now."

Rex's tail swept back and forth, swishing the dusty path. "I've been up here since lunchtime sniffing around after rabbits. I didn't catch any," he added quickly.

Polly nodded. She wasn't even sure he could catch them – he certainly couldn't eat them if he did. As a ghost dog, Rex didn't really need to eat, although he loved trying.

"Ah, there she is." Rex glanced back along the path. "Your mother is here."

Polly followed his look and saw to her surprise that he was right. Her mum was walking along the path, carrying a big beach bag. Polly could see towels poking out of the top. "Mum!" she called, waving. "What are you doing here?"

Her mum waved back and hurried to meet her. "Oh, Polly, I'm glad I found you! I was going to collect you from school, but then one of the volunteers called me down to the ticket office and I didn't leave on time. So I just hoped I'd meet you on the way home instead. I thought we could go to the beach together. It feels like I haven't seen you all week now you're back at school. I've got a picnic…" She waggled the bag temptingly.

"Will you come swimming with me?" Polly asked hopefully.

"Absolutely. So, how was today?"

Polly nibbled her top lip. "Better," she said at last.

Her mum looked down at her. "Really? Oh, Poll, I'm so glad."

Polly stopped and glared at her suspiciously. "But I told you it was fine!"

Beside her Rex gave a tiny, disbelieving snort and Polly had to fight not to poke him in the ribs. He was always trying to make her laugh in front of people. Sometimes it wasn't fair, having an invisible dog.

"Yes, but you didn't sound fine." Polly's mum led the way as they headed along the cliff. "I was worried about you. I thought you could be just putting on a brave face. Today you actually sound as though things might be better. Which is excellent."

Polly sighed. Occasionally her mum was altogether too clever.

"So what was good about today?" Mum asked, as they started to thread their way down one of the sandy paths that led to the cove.

"Well, you know that girl Lucy that we met at the uniform shop?"

"Uh-huh, you're sitting next to her, you told me."

"Today Lucy and I got made partners for our history topic and then we hung around at break together. I felt like we were friends." Polly paused for a moment. "I told her about Dad," she said eventually. "I'd never told anybody before." That wasn't completely true, but almost.

"Oh, Polly. That was brave of you. Was it… Was it all right?"

"Mmmm. It felt good that someone at school knew. And that's weird because I really didn't want people making a fuss, like they used to at Park Road."

"That's really good." Her mum blinked and then eyed Polly hopefully. "Did you say a *history* project?"

Polly laughed. "I knew you wouldn't be able to resist! It's on the Second World War. We were talking about evacuees this afternoon. Mum, I just remembered, Lizzie told me that the toy dog in the nursery belonged to a girl who was evacuated here. It's … weird."

Her mum nodded. "I know what you mean. It's hard to imagine, all those children being moved away from their families. Did Lizzie tell you about the shelter?"

Polly shook her head. "No… Is there one here? Why did they even need a shelter? Penhallow's not near a city."

"I think it was because of being close to some big harbours that were used by the Navy," her mum explained. "And actually I don't think it was ever used very much."

"Where was it? Was it an Anderson shelter? Miss Roberts told us about those – that you had to bury them in the garden and then people grew vegetables over the top."

"No, it's indoors. Somewhere in the cellars, close to the kitchens I think." Polly's mum frowned, trying to remember. "I'll see if I can find out for you. The house is so massive, there are still bits I haven't been to, and I'm supposed to be in charge of the whole place."

"Thanks, Mum. Would it be OK to invite Lucy round after school one day? She's really nice."

"Of course you can!" Polly's mum kissed the top of her head and reached for the bag. "Come on, we'll swim first and then have our picnic. I've got my costume on underneath – here's yours."

Polly wriggled into her costume under her towel and then dragged her mum behind her towards the sea, which was hissing and foaming against the sand of the beach. The waves were so tiny they were hardly there, nothing more than little ripples creeping towards their toes.

"Oh, it's cold!" Polly's mum shuddered, stepping back. "Perhaps I'll just watch."

"Mu-um! You promised." Polly glared at her.

"I thought the water was supposed to get warmer towards the end of the summer." Her mum stepped in a little further and made a face.

"It's going to be dark before you actually get in the sea," Polly pointed out, and giggled as Rex bounded past, playing chase with the little waves.

Polly woke early on Saturday morning as the September sun shone in through her round window. She blinked in the golden light and smiled. She was excited about inviting Lucy over one day. She loved her strange, quirky little tower room and it would be good to show it to a friend – a living, breathing friend. William was good company, when he was around, but ghosts didn't seem to have the same sense of time. He was there when he was there and there was no arguing with it.

She stretched her arms up above her head,

enjoying that lazy weekend feeling. It was still really early – she didn't *have* to get up. But she wasn't sleepy any more.

What should she do today? It was obviously going to be sunny, so the gardens would be busy and the cove, too. Mum was on duty so they couldn't go out for the day but Polly didn't mind. She decided she was looking forward to just mooching around the house and spending some time with Rex.

The dog from the nursery was in the back of her mind, niggling at her. Why was he so sad? Who was he missing? Polly yawned and decided that she was properly awake now. She'd been planning to go back to sleep, but she wanted to go and see him – just not on her own this time.

She stumbled out of bed and went to look in her wardrobe. She'd been wearing school uniform all week – she was going to wear something she really liked. Shorts, maybe – it was still warm enough. She grabbed a pair of cropped dungarees and a yellow top, and got dressed, then crept quietly through the living room since Mum was still asleep. She headed down the tower steps to the main house and the terrace.

Rex shook himself when she ran her hand along his spine and the rich gold of his coat shimmered over the grey stone. He leaned down and licked her cheek. "You look … determined," he said, eyeing her. Then he glanced around the gardens and snorted. "Very determined. What is it, five in the morning?"

"More like six. Will you come up to the nursery with me?" Polly asked. "I can't stop thinking about that toy dog."

Rex blinked in surprise, but he nodded and jumped down off his plinth. "I can't either. I didn't even know he was there..." he murmured, as Polly followed him up the main stairs. "Not until Magnus mentioned him. How could I have forgotten? And a child mixed up in the story, too..."

Polly frowned at the carvings on the banisters as she considered her answer. She had thought she was imagining it, the first time she saw them move, but now she was sure – the little wooden dogs carved in and out of the banister posts, and peeping out from under the handrail were definitely moving. They stirred as Rex passed, ears twitching, tails swishing. She wondered how old they were, the dogs that watched her now. Mum had told her that the earliest part of the house that still stood had been built by a courtier to Henry VIII but the banisters were even older than that. They had been taken out of the medieval Penhallow Hall before it was knocked down to build the beautiful Tudor house.

"When Magnus talked about him, he said the dog was lonely," she muttered, thinking it over. "What if we could help? Like we did with Li-Mei?"

Rex nosed her gently. "A good thought."

They paced together along the passage that led to the old nurseries and servants' bedrooms, and Polly peered carefully in to make sure no one was there. Early morning sunlight shone on the wooden floorboards and the faded old rocking horse creaked faintly, as though a child had only just climbed down from his back.

"This dog," Rex murmured, peering up at the toy. "Do I remember him?" The dog's paws were saggy and it sat on the shelf as though it really was nothing more than a battered old toy. But Polly knew that wasn't true – she had felt the dog's sadness so strongly a few days before.

"Do you remember all the dogs?" Polly asked curiously, and Rex's ears twitched.

"Once I would have said yes, of course… But when my people left, something happened to me – I still don't know what. I remember Magnus, and playing with him and William on the lawns and in the cove. But he was the last true child of Penhallow, the last child I remember loving. After that … it seems I was sleeping too deeply." He licked Polly's hand. "Until you."

He stretched up, suddenly towering over Polly with his front paws up against the wall so that he could sniff at the toy dog on the shelf. It slipped as he nudged it, slumping down in a heap, its glass eye staring foolishly.

Rex nosed at it again, his ears flickering with impatience, and then gently pushed the toy off the shelf so that Polly could catch it.

Polly cradled the worn old dog, expecting to feel some rush of life inside it, even if it didn't truly wake, but there was nothing. Or … perhaps there was some life there but the dog had shut itself away. Polly had the sense that it didn't want to be woken.

"I don't know if we should do this," she said to Rex suddenly, stretching up her hands to return the toy dog to the shelf.

Rex let out a breath of a growl and nudged her hands back. "Magnus was right – this dog is desperately lonely. I can feel the sadness in him – it's making my claws ache. He needs to wake and run again. We should take him to the cove, and let him chase in and out of the waves. He has been alone up here for too long."

"But if he doesn't want to wake up…"

"Then we shall have to make him," Rex said sternly. He licked the toy dog's ear and Polly flinched. She knew the toy wasn't valuable but he was still part of the house's collection. His ear was definitely a bit slobbery now, although that didn't seem to have encouraged him to wake up.

"He's resisting," Rex muttered. "You try, Polly. You woke me and Li-Mei. Perhaps it needs a child to call him back."

Please… Polly whispered to the dog in her head. *Come and talk to us. We're worried about you. Can't we help?*

There was nothing – not even a no. Polly

tried again, reaching out to him. *Perhaps we could make you feel better? We could play with you!* She tried to think of things that the dog would like to do – walks and swimming and chasing after a ball.

NO!

She almost dropped him. The dog was there, all of a sudden, in her head and in her arms, too, a scruffy little terrier wriggling furiously in her grip. Polly put him down hastily, and he glared up at her and Rex. He was clearly angry, but one of his ears kept flopping over, and he looked so sweet that Polly wanted to laugh.

"Go away and leave me alone," he snarled, and then his bright black eyes glazed over and once again he was a saggy old toy, slumped on the floor.

Rex stretched out one paw to nudge him gently but there was nothing there. The wolfhound shuddered and leaned heavily against Polly. For once, Polly felt as though she was giving him her strength and not the other way around.

4

A Visitor to Penhallow

"Lucy, I could hear you singing along, that was beautiful. We'll all be learning 'We'll Meet Again' to sing to your parents on the Open Afternoon," Miss Roberts added, as she stopped the video. "It's one of the most popular wartime songs."

Polly glanced at Lucy and couldn't help grinning. Lucy and Martha had told her on the first day that they'd be doing something like this. They'd spent the morning writing diary entries for children who'd been evacuated from cities to the countryside, and Polly had found it heartbreaking. Miss Roberts had read them some letters she'd found online from children back to their parents, begging to be allowed to come home. That was sad enough, but Polly kept thinking of the toy dog up in the nursery.

She and Rex had not gone back there – Polly had spent Sunday with her mum, going on a walk to see another beautiful beach. On the way home she'd stopped by Rex's statue to stroke him but that was all. Even just patting him, she could tell he was upset. He had been strangely silent ever since the little dog in the nursery had refused to talk to them. Polly was sure that he was feeling guilty – that he thought he should have done more to help. She would go and talk to him today, after school.

"Right, that's the bell for lunch. We'll carry on talking about wartime songs afterwards,"

Miss Roberts called, as everyone jumped up.

"I'm starving." Lucy sighed. Then she jumped sideways. "Ow!"

Martha turned round, looking innocent. "What?"

"You pinched me!"

Martha rolled her eyes. "Don't be stupid. Of course I didn't."

"Yes you did! Why do you have to be so horrible?" Lucy demanded, and Polly moved up closer to her, standing next to her to stare back at Martha.

"You think you're so special!" Martha snapped back. "Sucking up to Miss Roberts all the time! Well, you needn't think Polly's going to want to be friends with you! No one does!" Then she flounced away, leaving Polly staring after her.

"What was all that about?" she murmured, but Lucy didn't answer – and when Polly turned to look at her, she saw that she was crying. Not noisily, but there were tears spilling down the side of her nose.

"Lucy! Are you all right?" Miss Roberts stopped to look at them anxiously, and Polly wondered if she should tell her that Martha had pinched Lucy. But Lucy was gripping on to Polly's hand, as if she was trying to pass on a message.

Polly tried to smile at Miss Roberts. "It's her hayfever."

Miss Roberts nodded slowly – Polly wasn't sure the teacher was convinced but she obviously decided to let it go. "You'd better get to lunch. Roast dinner day – you don't want to miss out on Yorkshire pudding."

Polly nodded and hurriedly steered Lucy down the corridor and into the lunch queue.

"You might have to pretend to sneeze for a bit. Sorry, I couldn't think of anything else to say, and you did look a bit like my mum when the tree pollen comes out. Please don't cry! Come on, let's have some lunch."

She looked worriedly at Lucy, who was still sniffing. "Hey, how much do you want to bet Miss Roberts is going to get the dinner ladies to make wartime lunches? Like the rationing she was talking about, with everything being made with powdered eggs and carrots instead of sugar."

"Carrots?" Lucy half hiccupped. "That can't be right. S'disgusting."

"Carrots, she definitely said so. But they can't have been like, in tea, can they?" Polly wittered on, trying to think of anything she could say to cheer her up. It didn't seem to be working very well, but at least Lucy wasn't actually crying when Martha wandered past their table, obviously looking to see if she was upset.

She didn't talk much for the rest of lunch, though, and by the time the bell went for afternoon lessons, Polly was exhausted from trying to be cheerful. Still, Lucy *was* grateful. When they sat down in the classroom again, she took the little dog key ring off her rucksack and shoved it into Polly's hand.

"Here. Thanks."

"You don't need to – don't start crying again!" Polly hissed. "OK, look, I'll put it on my bag. It's really cute."

It looked like the little white dog, Polly realized sadly, remembering him squirming furiously in her arms.

Lucy was very silent all afternoon but Polly put that down to Miss Roberts asking them to revise fractions. Fractions would shut anybody up. Polly was planning to talk to Lucy after school – maybe they could even walk down to look at the boats in the harbour. Mum had told her that as long as she was back at Penhallow by half past four, it was fine to hang about and chat with people after school. But by the time she'd grabbed her jacket and headed out to the gate, Lucy was gone.

Polly looked around for her, hurrying a little way down the road towards where she thought

Lucy had told her she lived, but there was no sign of her at all. With a sigh, she headed back towards the path across the cliffs.

It was as she was walking along the path that she heard the noise. A little whining sound. A seagull, maybe. She looked out over the metal rail that ran along the edge of the path, searching the sea. Today the water was a soft greenish brown, waves slapping lightly at the beach below. But there were no gulls.

Polly stood on the path, looking around uncertainly. The whining came again and there was a rustling among the brambles that grew on the other side of the path. Maybe it was a dog? A lost dog on the path? Her heart thumped excitedly as she remembered Stephen asking her to look out for a little white dog.

"Hey…" she called, rather doubtfully. "Are you hiding?"

Nothing – only silence. But it was a listening sort of silence and Polly was almost sure that something was there.

After a few seconds she called out again. This time there was a definite rustling and Polly realized that something was coming towards her through the brambles. Something quite big. Perhaps the dog had been bigger than Stephen thought – after all, he had only seen it from a distance...

Then Lucy scrambled out of the thicket in front of her and stood up, brushing at her scratched arms and making a face.

"It's you!" Polly squeaked.

"Er, yes..."

"What were you doing in there?" Polly demanded. "I thought you were a dog!"

"What?" Lucy yelped, a flash of fear darting across her face. "What do you mean?"

Polly frowned. "I heard a whining noise.
It definitely sounded like a dog. And Stephen
– he's the Head Gardener up at the house –
I told you about the little white dog he saw
running across the lawn the other day. He
reckoned it was a stray. He asked me to keep
an eye out. I thought maybe the dog was in
those brambles…"

"I haven't seen a stray dog today," Lucy said
firmly, shaking her head.

"OK. So … what were you doing?" Polly asked. "And what was that weird whining…" She trailed off, suddenly realizing what it must have been. She'd thought that Lucy was feeling better but she'd hidden herself away to cry.

Polly hesitated. If it were her, she'd hate it if someone heard her crying. She'd want them to hurry on by and pretend they hadn't noticed. Lucy must have come here because the path wasn't that busy. She hadn't expected anyone to walk past – she'd just wanted a quiet, private place to be sad.

"Oh, sorry… Were you crying?"

Lucy hesitated for a moment, looking confused, and then she nodded. "Um. Yes."

Polly crouched down to look, and noticed that the brambles and gorse bushes had grown into a little tunnel, like a hidey-hole. Perhaps it had been worn away by rabbits or foxes, she decided. It looked like there was some sort of tumbledown building a few metres in – the brambles must have grown up around it.

"Is this your hiding place? Have you been here before?"

"I found it ages ago," Lucy explained, still looking anxious. "I like it. It's quiet. No one ever knows I'm here."

"Sorry… I didn't mean to spoil it."

Lucy shrugged. "I'm all right, you know," she said. Then she looked back worriedly at the brambles and the old shed. "I've got to go home. It's almost dinner time."

"Oh, OK. Um, wait… Do you want to come back to my house?"

"Your house?"

"My flat, I mean." Polly took a deep breath and looked at her nervously, hoping she wouldn't say no. "We're halfway there," she pointed out. "You might as well. Mum won't mind. I asked her the other day if it was OK for you to come over."

"My gran…" Lucy started, looking back at the little stone building as though she wasn't sure what to do. "She won't know where I am."

"You could ring her," Polly suggested.

"OK. Um, yes, I suppose I could. I've got my mobile."

"Wow, you've got your own phone? My mum says I don't need one till secondary school."

Lucy nodded. "My mum bought it for me." She shrugged and gave Polly a tiny smile. "So that I can call her when I'm staying with my dad. But it's useful – it means I don't always have to go straight home from school. Gran's fine with that, as long as I let her know where I am." She sighed. "I rang her when I got out of school and told her I was going to Martha's.

She knows Martha and her mum, so I knew she wouldn't mind…"

Polly made a face. "Will she be OK about you coming to mine?"

"I'll ring her and say I've gone to yours instead." Lucy was still looking a bit doubtful but she walked with Polly along the path until they could see the house. "I can't believe you live here!"

"Only in a bit of it. That tower, on the end. You have to get to it from the first floor. Off the gallery round the main stairs, you know?"

Lucy shook her head. "I've never been there."

"But you live so close!" Polly stared at her.

"I know… My dad was never into big houses and you have to pay." She looked worried for a minute. "I haven't got any money on me."

"It's all right, you won't have to buy a ticket. You don't think I have to pay every time I go in, do you?"

Lucy smiled faintly at her. "No, I suppose not. It *is* beautiful," she added, as they walked across the lawn.

"I can show you around if you like? I know all the good bits."

Lucy actually laughed. "OK. What are the good bits?"

The dogs… Polly swallowed. Her personal

tour of Penhallow would be all the dogs, she realized. Li-Mei in the Red Drawing Room. Rex and Magnus on either side of the terrace steps. The gorgeous little greyhound peeping round Lady Augusta's skirt in the portrait in the salon. The silver dog on the butter dish that was set out on the enormous dining table. Lucy loved dogs as much as she did. Polly was almost sure that she wouldn't be able to see Rex and the others – after all, the house was full of children visiting and they never saw anything. But there was something about Lucy…

Lucy was looking at her curiously and Polly gave her a hurried smile. "I really like the nursery. There's a huge doll's house – it's amazing. It's got everything. Even tiny little plates with food on."

Lucy's face lit up. "My mum loves doll's

houses." She went pink. "She even helps me make stuff for mine sometimes." She looked sideways at Polly.

"Lucky! Is it big? I had a tiny one but I never liked playing with it that much. It didn't have any stairs and it just seemed a bit weird. I mean how were they ever supposed to get from floor to floor?" Polly shook her head. "Don't laugh!" she added, even though she was sniggering, too. It did suddenly seem really funny.

"Martha said having a doll's house was babyish."

"Yeah, well." Polly shrugged. "Martha's like that, isn't she?"

Lucy stared at her and then smiled. "Mm. I s'pose you're right."

"She's nice."

Polly tried not to jump. Rex had appeared out of the shrubbery next to her, peering curiously at Lucy. Polly smiled at him – she couldn't talk back to him silently, the way he could to her.

"We'd better go and tell my mum we're here. And then if she's OK with you staying you can phone your gran," Polly said, giving Rex a quick warning scowl, which only made him wag his tail. She led Lucy into the house through one of the side doors and then through the door marked 'Private' that led to the offices. She put her head round the door to the manager's office and beamed at her mum.

"Is it all right if Lucy stays for dinner? This is Lucy," she added, stepping back to show Lucy hovering behind her.

"Oh! Of course it is – it's only sausages though, I haven't got anything special," Polly's mum said apologetically.

"I love sausages," Lucy said, a little shyly. "Thank you for having me."

"I'm going to show Lucy around," Polly said.

"Great. I'll go and put dinner on."

"Sausages." Rex sighed in Polly's ear. "You could feed me just half a sausage, couldn't you, lovely Polly? I miss sausages."

"You don't eat!" Polly whispered back.

"I could try…"

Polly took Lucy around the house, trying to remember all the things that the guides pointed out. Lucy seemed to love the same things she did, though. She cooed over the greyhound in Lady Augusta's portrait. "You can see how soft his fur is," she murmured, standing on tiptoe to look at it better. "I love this painting. You're so lucky to live here!"

Polly grinned at her. "You haven't seen our actual flat yet. It's pretty tiny. Actually, I bet dinner's ready. Come on."

Sitting round the table with Mum and Lucy felt so good, Polly decided, squeezing more ketchup on to her sausages. It was ages since she'd had a friend round, even before they'd come to Penhallow. Rex was sitting next to Polly's chair, occasionally sniffing mournfully at the sausages he couldn't eat.

Polly's mum dug out a packet of biscuits for

pudding and then sighed. "I ought to go and do a bit more work."

"I should get back home," Lucy said, looking at her watch and jumping up.

"You haven't seen the doll's house!"

"Oh… Um, yes. Just for a bit then." Lucy looked at her watch again and Polly wondered why she was suddenly in a hurry.

Polly saw Rex's ears lie flat as he watched them walking along the gallery to the other staircase and realized that they were heading for the nursery. They hadn't been back since the toy dog had told them to go away and she knew Rex was still worrying about it. He saw the dog's unhappiness as something that he had done wrong, Polly was sure. He had failed to take care of one of his own.

As they walked round the gallery, Lucy ran her fingers over the carvings on the rail, smiling at the little faces peeping out at her.

"She sees the carved dogs," Rex whispered
to Polly. "Most people don't notice them, you
know. I like her." He paced closer to Lucy,
ghosting underneath her hand as they climbed
the stairs so that she stroked his ears.

Polly saw Lucy lift her hand in surprise, staring at her fingers.

She nodded to Rex, smiling as she led the way up to the nursery corridor. "This is the nursery," she told Lucy. "We're lucky there's no one here – everyone loves the doll's house." She was talking about the doll's house but she couldn't help looking sideways at the toy dog on his shelf. He was still there, of course, slumped and silent. Polly flicked her eyes back to Lucy.

"Wow! It's huge…"

"That china on the dining table is Royal Doulton," Polly told her. She'd heard the volunteers tell people so many times. "The factories made special miniature sets for children to play with."

"I can't imagine playing with a house like this," Lucy said, crouching down to examine the kitchen. "It's all so delicate. I mean, what if you broke one of those dolls? They're all china."

"I know. But I suppose if you had a doll's house like this, your parents could afford new dolls." Polly sighed. "Sometimes they let me help dust it, and even that makes me feel panicky."

They peered into the doll's house. As Lucy got back to her feet she caught sight of the toy dog, lying on his shelf. "Oh, look," she murmured, reaching up to pet his balding nose. Then she pulled her hand back guiltily. "Sorry! I forgot we're not allowed to touch. I just … really wanted to stroke him. I know it's silly – he's a toy – but he looked like his fur would be so nice to stroke." She looked wistfully up at the little dog and then blinked, glancing at Polly as though she'd said something stupid. "Sorry, I know that sounds mad."

Polly realized that she'd been staring and
shook her head. "It doesn't!" Had the dog
woken up for Lucy? Just for a second? She
hadn't seen him but it seemed that Lucy had, or
that something about the dog had called to her.

"I'd better go, Polly, sorry," Lucy muttered.
"I told Gran I'd be back after tea." Then she
shook her head and seemed to speak without
thinking. "He's got the same colour fur."

"What?" Polly asked, and Lucy stared at her in horror.

"Nothing! No one, I mean. I don't know what I'm talking about. I really need to get home, sorry."

Polly looked back over her shoulder as they went to the door. The toy dog had moved, she was sure of it. He had turned his head to look at them – to look at Lucy. His one glass eye shone with life as he watched her go.

5

The Photograph

Polly walked Lucy back to her gran's house, with a very quick look at the terrace on the way to the cliff path. Rex's statue wasn't there, of course, since he was following them around, sniffing curiously at Lucy every so often, but Lucy patted Magnus and stroked his carved ears.

"My statue is much more handsome," Rex grumbled to Polly. "She should have seen me. She is a good friend for you, this one. She knows how to stroke a dog well, look at her. I can almost see Magnus grinning."

They strolled back along the cliff path together, Polly watching Rex bound in front of them, snuffling among the brambles for rabbits and snapping at butterflies.

"You don't need to come all the way home with me," Lucy said, after a couple of minutes. "I can go on my own from here."

"I don't mind." Polly shrugged. "I haven't got anything else to do."

Lucy looked around, biting her bottom lip, and Polly stared at her. What had happened? Why was she suddenly all uptight? They were back at the same bit of the path where she'd found Lucy earlier on, the little tunnel through the brambles by the ruined stone shed. "Are you embarrassed about crying?" she asked awkwardly. "You shouldn't be."

"No," Lucy murmured. She cast a worried sort of look at the shed and then sped up.

"It's just that I'm so late. Come on!"

Polly nodded and didn't argue. She still reckoned Lucy was embarrassed, whatever she said. She looked back at the little tumbledown shed one last time as they carried on down the path, wondering how much time Lucy had spent worrying to herself in that secret hiding place. She caught her breath.

For just a second, she'd thought that there was a little face gazing out at her from the battered window – a little, whiskery, whitish-grey face. Then she blinked and it was gone. Polly shook her head and ran after Lucy.

When they got back to the road, Lucy waved towards a lane leading away from the village. "The house is down there."

They went on down the lane, past grey stone cottages that looked to Polly as though they should be on a calendar or jigsaw puzzle.

They were too pretty to be actually lived in.

"I love the thatched roofs," she told Lucy, stopping to stare.

"Mmm. They're OK." Lucy shrugged. "I think there's mice in ours. My bedroom's right under the roof and it's all scrabbly."

"You live in one of these?" Polly looked at her in surprise. "Wow."

"You can't be jealous, you live in a stately home!"

"A very tiny bit of one."

"This is Gran's house. I don't know if I told you, me and Mum moved in with her after she and Dad split." Lucy stopped at a little wooden gate that led into a garden full of foxgloves and roses that were gently dropping their last petals. It was beautiful. She pointed up at a little window in the thatch. "That's my bedroom."

"You're back!" A thin, grey-haired lady came round the side of the cottage and smiled at them. "I was starting to worry about you. Hello, Polly."

"Hi." Polly smiled back shyly.

"Lucy's said how nice it's been having you at school. You'll have to come round for tea one day – I'm sure Lucy's mum would like to meet you, too. She's still at work at the moment – she does long shifts, you see."

Polly smiled. "That would be great. See you tomorrow, Lucy!"

She looked back as she was walking down the lane. Lucy was talking to her gran – she had her arm round Lucy's shoulders and was pointing at the roses climbing up the cottage wall. Lucy was smiling but she still looked worried about something. Polly just wished that her friend would tell her what it was.

"Polly, could you take this to Mrs Jones for me?" Miss Roberts handed Polly a folder. "You know where her office is, don't you?"

Polly nodded. She had been at the school for more than a week now and it wasn't very big. She was pretty sure she knew where everything was. She headed down the corridor towards the head's office. The door was open and Mrs Jones was on the phone. She smiled at Polly and mouthed, "Wait a minute!"

Polly lingered in the corridor, looking at the old school photos on the wall. Most of them were only from twenty or thirty years before but they still looked ancient – it was something about the hairstyles, Polly decided, peering at them closely.

There were a few black and white photos that were clearly much older than the others, and she stretched up on tiptoe to read the label on one just above her head. *Infant Class Christmas, 1939.* A row of solemn-looking children, seated tidily on a bench and staring at the camera. Polly couldn't tear herself away from it – the round, babyish faces, the little girls' hair tied back in ribbons, the boys in long socks and shorts, even in the winter.

"Are you all right, Polly? I called... Oh, you're looking at the photographs. Aren't they fascinating?" Mrs Jones came to stand next to her and Polly handed her the folder.

"I'm sorry, I didn't hear you! Mrs Jones, would these have been the evacuees?"

"Some of them were, yes, I'm sure. Did Miss Roberts tell you about them? You're learning about the Second World War, aren't you?"

"Yes, but it was actually someone at Penhallow Hall who told me there'd been evacuees there. I just wondered if they were in this photo – I hadn't thought that they would have been at this school." She looked again at the faces. There was one little girl gazing back at her so sadly. She seemed somehow familiar. Then Polly realized it wasn't the child she knew – it was the toy dog clutched in her lap. A much-loved saggy stuffed dog, the same one that was up on a shelf in the nursery. And the boy next to the little girl, his hand protectively over hers, had to be the girl's older brother.

At Mrs Jones's suggestion, Polly took the
photograph back to the classroom to show
Miss Roberts, who passed it round delightedly.

"You're like a detective, Polly! I had wondered
if any evacuee children came to our school but
I hadn't thought of looking at the photos."

"It was an accident. I was just waiting
for Mrs Jones." Polly ducked her head,
embarrassed.

Miss Roberts propped up the photo against

some books on her desk. Polly couldn't stop looking at it. The evacuee girl's eyes almost seemed to follow her around.

"That's the dog, isn't it?" Lucy asked, later that afternoon when they were meant to be planning out their poems.

Polly blinked at her. "Which dog?" she asked slowly.

"The dog up in the nursery, the one I stroked. That's him in the picture."

"Yeah, I think so."

"So that little girl was an evacuee to your house?" Lucy's blue eyes seemed wider and darker than Polly had noticed them being before.

"What's the matter?" Polly whispered.

"Nothing… I just hate to think of them, going off on those trains. Not knowing where they'd be sleeping that night. And some of them were so little! That girl, she can't have been more than five, Polly. She looks so sad. Just imagine it. They must have felt like they didn't belong anywhere any more, that they didn't have a home."

"I know what you mean," Polly murmured, thinking of those first strange days at Penhallow, before she met Rex.

Polly turned over in bed and sighed. She'd been trying to get to sleep for ages but it wasn't going to happen. There was too much going round and round in her head. She kept thinking about the evacuee children. She was worried about Lucy, too. What had she really been doing up on the cliff path? Because now that Polly thought about it, she didn't look as though she'd been crying. She'd just been jumpy. There was definitely something going on and it wasn't just Martha being mean.

Polly sat up. She couldn't help Lucy now but at least she could do something for Rex. He was still feeling guilty about the toy dog in the nursery. He hadn't realized that the dog was so lonely and sad when he should have known all the dogs at Penhallow.

Polly wasn't sure that the toy dog would wake up and talk to her properly. But even if he didn't, she could talk to him. Perhaps the words would seep through. She could explain, apologize, beg him to talk to Rex. She could tell him that maybe they could help. She could make things better both for the toy dog and for Rex, the way Rex had made things so much better for her.

When she'd got back from school, Polly had borrowed Mum's book on the history of Penhallow Hall, hoping to find out some more about the house during the Second World War. There wasn't a lot to read, though. None of the people who lived in the house after the Penhallow family had left had seemed to make much of a mark on the place. There was a brief description of the two sisters that Lizzie had talked about, Mrs Ford and Miss Laleham, saying that they had moved in together after Mrs Ford's husband had been sent overseas. There was a photo of the two of them standing on the terrace and one of the inside of the air-raid shelter, with several beds, but that was about it. The book didn't mention evacuees at all. Polly had tried asking Mum again – she had the brilliant excuse that it was for school.

"Oh, yes, that little dog. Lizzie told me that story, too. It's so sad, thinking of those poor children. I don't know much else, Polly, to be honest. There's an old accounts book we found, which mentions buying children's clothes, but that's about it. I don't think they stayed very long – certainly not all through the war. Sorry not to be more help, love."

Polly didn't know where to look next. It seemed that her only source of information was going to be the dog himself – and that wasn't looking very hopeful. Still, she was going to try. She couldn't bear the droop of Rex's tail.

But when she arrived at the nursery, padding through the corridors with a hoodie pulled on over her pyjamas, William and Magnus were already there. William was curled up in an old basketwork chair with Magnus draped across his feet.

"Did you know I was coming?" she asked, puzzled. She had never understood how William and his ghost dog understood when to appear.

William shrugged. "*Something* was going to happen." Then he looked past her to the door of the nursery and Polly turned.

Rex was there, looking shyly around the door as if he wasn't sure he was welcome.

"I didn't come and find you because I was going to try and talk to him," Polly explained. "You were so miserable when he turned us away, I didn't want to make you try again."

"But I have to." Rex sighed, pacing towards her. "It's what I am, Polly. He's one of mine." Rex sat down beside her, and looked up at the dog on the shelf. "I can't leave him now, however much he wants me to."

"I do want you to." The white dog was there, staring down at them and growling. He jumped from the shelf to the back of an armchair and glared. Even huge Rex took a step back. "Can't you see I want to be left alone?"

"Dogs are pack animals." Rex shook himself. "We belong together. You're a Penhallow dog."

"I wasn't here long enough for that. I don't belong to you."

Rex let out an angry huff. "It isn't about belonging – or it is, but not *to* me. You're a part of us, the dogs of Penhallow. We're together, we're all stronger that way. You can't deny that you're lonely."

"I'm lonely because I choose to be. I didn't want you to wake me up and make me talk." The white dog turned away from Rex and stared at Polly. "Why are you here?"

"I thought you were unhappy…" Polly faltered. "I wanted to help. And Rex hates that you're so alone, can't you see that?"

"It isn't any of his business. Who was that other girl?"

Polly blinked in surprise and then nodded to herself. So he *had* woken up when Lucy was there. "She's a friend from school and she came home with me. She noticed you. Did you feel her? She patted your nose."

"Maybe." The dog hunched himself up, surly and still half growling. "What's her name?"

Polly sat down on the floor in front of the armchair, settling herself comfortably. "I'll tell you her name if you tell me why you don't want us to talk to you."

The dog growled again, the fur lifting along the back of his neck as he paced the top of the chair. "And then you'll go away and leave me alone?"

Polly didn't really want to agree but if the dog wouldn't talk, they'd never be able to find a way to help him. "Yes." She felt the floorboards creak and give as Rex settled himself beside her.

"I came here from a farm, not that far away. I was only small. Smaller than I am now." The white dog eyed Magnus and Rex, as though he was a little jealous of their size, but then he scrabbled his way down the back of the chair, and settled on the cushions. "I was given to them. Jack and Annie. They had just arrived here, too, and they were as confused about it all as I was."

"Were they the evacuee children?" Polly asked gently.

All three dogs looked at her uncertainly as though they didn't know the word. William didn't look very sure either.

Polly hesitated. "I mean, they came to Penhallow from a city? To get away from the bombs?"

"Yes." The white dog was silent for a moment. "Miss went and got me to cheer them up. They didn't like it here."

"How could they not?" Rex lifted his head to stare, puzzled. Penhallow was part of him – he expected everyone to love it as he did.

"Well, they left their family behind," Polly pointed out. "And Miss Roberts said that lots of the children didn't like being in the country. Some of them had never seen farm animals before. Everything was different."

Rex grunted doubtfully but didn't argue.

"What about the toy dog?" Polly asked. "Did that belong to Jack and Annie, too?"

"He was Annie's," the white dog agreed. "She brought him with her when they came. He was always just Dog before, but when I came along, we shared a name. I was Skip and so she named her toy dog after me. She loved him. Jack and Annie loved us both, even though they were unhappy here." He turned himself round, curling into a small white ball so that all Polly could see was the smooth curve of his back.

"What happened?" she whispered, after a moment. She didn't want to know, but she had to ask. It was like touching a wobbly tooth that was almost out.

"They went back."

"But – but they shouldn't have done!" Polly

protested. "There were bombs, they were there to be safe."

"Annie cried all the time." The little dog's voice was muffled in the cushions and the others had to lean closer to hear. "She used to cry into my fur – and her toy dog's. Her father came and took them both away, back to their real home."

"What about you?" Polly's voice shook.

"They lived in a flat. No room for a dog. They wanted to keep me but their father wouldn't let them. Miss had to take me away in the end to stop the children crying. She shut me up in one of the stables because I wouldn't stop howling. And Annie must have dropped the toy dog when her father was carrying her away. She was crying so much – she couldn't have told him."

"And that was it? You never saw them again?"

"I got out of the stables." He peered at her over his shoulder. "There was a loose board. I worried at it and scratched at it and I got out, but by then they were gone."

His head sank down again and Polly leaned her arms on the chair to listen closer. Rex was pressed up against her, and Magnus and William were crouched by the arm of the chair, all of them intent on the story. "I followed their scent. I was good at that. I followed them all along the road. Jack, and their father carrying Annie. I stood where they stood, on the side of the road. And then it went away. I lost it."

"Maybe they caught a bus," William suggested in a whisper. "What did you do?"

"Went on," muttered the dog. "In case I found them again. But I never did."

"You just kept walking?" Polly swallowed hard.

"Mmm." The dog let out a shuddery little sigh. "I don't know. There was a car. I ran out into the road – I thought perhaps it was them…"

Polly and William exchanged horrified glances, and Rex pulled away from Polly to nuzzle at the little dog.

"I bet they always remembered you," Polly whispered at last. "They really loved you."

"And you came back here, to be with us," Rex growled. "You're a Penhallow dog, like it or not."

6

A Dream from the Past

Polly sat curled in the armchair in the nursery, with Rex stretched out asleep at her feet. She knew she should go back to the flat and get ready for bed but she had too much thinking to do. Skip's story had been so unbelievably sad and he was so lonely.

Polly kept remembering the way he and Lucy had been drawn together. There was something about the two of them – it was as if they needed each other. Even though Lucy put a brave face on it, Polly was pretty sure she was still upset about her dad not being around.

And she had Martha picking on her as well. Maybe Lucy needed a dog to make her feel better, just like Jack and Annie had? If only Polly could bring Skip and Lucy together. If Skip thought that someone needed him again, perhaps he wouldn't insist on staying shut away with his memories any more.

Jack and Annie had adored Skip – Polly had been able to tell that from the way the little dog had told his story. And he had loved them back. He must have helped to make those strange few months at Penhallow a little less frightening for them.

Perhaps he might do it again? Polly smiled to herself, imagining Skip in Lucy's arms, licking her cheek. But it couldn't happen. Lucy wouldn't even be able to see him. She sighed, leaning back a little against the velvety cushion of the armchair. She mustn't sleep here…

She heard them before she saw them. High, excited voices and a yapping bark. Then they raced by her, under the tree. Jack in the lead, with Skip chasing him in a flurry of too-big puppy paws, and Annie following along behind, giggling to herself. She had a scruffy white toy dog dangling from her hand.

They didn't sound unhappy, Polly thought. In the bright sunshine on the lawn, it looked like the best kind of summer afternoon, laughing and messing about with your beloved puppy.

But then Annie tripped over as she scampered up the terrace steps and fell, scraping her knee on the stone. Polly watched, horrified, as she stumbled up and began to wail. She stood next to Rex's statue and howled.

Rex didn't wake up – Polly watched for a twitch of a stone ear or a flush of gold over his carved fur but there was nothing. How could he lie there and listen to the little girl cry?

Polly wanted to scramble down from the tree and run to Annie and hug her, but she knew she couldn't. She was the ghost here, not Annie and Jack and Skip.

But Rex – he could have helped. Or maybe not, Polly realized, digging her nails into her palms as Jack ran back to hug his little sister, and a lady in an old-fashioned flowered dress came hurrying down the steps to see what was the matter. This was only thirty years or so after William had died and the Penhallows had left the hall. Rex was lost without them – and for the first time in centuries, the spirit of Penhallow wasn't there to protect the children of his home.

"I want Mu-um. I want *my* mum, not you.
Go away!" Annie wailed, and the lady in the
flowered dress sighed and sat down on the
step below her, looking helpless. "I want to go
home!" Annie sobbed, as her brother cuddled
her close and whispered in her ear.

Polly knew what he was saying, even though
she couldn't hear him.

"Me, too."

When she got to school the next morning, Polly sneaked inside before they were meant to, desperate to look at the photograph again. It was back up on the wall in the corridor, so she was planning to say she'd needed the loo, if anyone asked. She wanted to see their faces.

She had no idea what had happened the night before – it was more than a dream, she was sure. It had been so real. Jack and Annie and Skip had been there, somehow. She lifted her hand to run her fingers over their solemn faces – and then the bell rang, loud and shrill, and she hurried away to her classroom.

The everyday school things shook the strangeness away and by the afternoon, the dream or vision or whatever it had been, had lost its power. Polly felt a part of things again. Enough to notice that Lucy was so jittery she could hardly sit still.

"What's the matter?" Polly whispered, leaning over to look at Lucy. "Did Martha say something to you again?"

Lucy blinked back at her and Polly sighed. It seemed like Lucy had only been half there all day. She had jumped out of her skin when Miss Roberts asked her a question earlier on and she'd hardly written anything in literacy.

Lucy was having a packed lunch but she'd not eaten much, just unwrapped her sandwiches and sausage roll and looked at them, then wrapped them up again. She ate her yoghurt and an apple but that was all. Polly had even given her a bit of her pizza from the school cafeteria, but although Lucy had said she wanted it, she'd put that away in her lunchbox, too. It was as though she was saving up food for a midnight feast.

She did join in afterwards, chasing around playing football with everyone else, but whenever they stopped for a rest, a faintly worried expression settled over her face. There was definitely something wrong.

"Lucy?" Polly asked again.

This time Lucy looked up and smiled. "I'm fine."

Polly sighed to herself but she couldn't make Lucy tell, could she? Perhaps they could talk properly after school, she wondered. Except she couldn't – Polly nibbled crossly on a fingernail, remembering. She had to stay when school was finished.

They'd had a note to take home earlier in the week, about a dance club after school that Miss Roberts and a dance teacher from another school were going to run. This term they were going to learn swing dancing, which had been popular during the Second World War. Polly had thought it sounded fun – and although she wasn't totally sure about an after-school club, not straight away, Mum had talked her into it. Lucy wasn't doing it – she said she was useless at dancing, she always tripped over.

She grabbed Lucy's arm as they went out to the cloakroom after school. "You are OK, aren't you?" Polly asked, turning pink at Lucy's surprised look. "You still look a bit out of it, that's all…" She shrugged helplessly.

"It's nothing. I promise." Lucy put her other arm round Polly's shoulders in half a hug. "Thanks for worrying about me. See you tomorrow!"

Polly nodded. "Yeah, see you tomorrow." She watched Lucy hurry out of the main door, almost running, she was so eager to get going. Martha – it had to be. But she hadn't noticed Martha anywhere near Lucy today. There was definitely something weird going on.

Polly grabbed her stuff and stalked along the corridor to the main hall, chewing on her thumbnail. It didn't help that Martha was in the hall, too, wearing some sort of special dancing shoes and doing warm-up exercises in a show-offy way.

Unfortunately, as the class began, Polly had to admit that Martha was a really good dancer. She seemed to get what they were being shown first time and she made it look easy. Polly felt as though she was always several steps behind, even though she was enjoying herself and she loved the catchy, bouncy music.

They stopped for a break halfway through and Martha drifted over to Polly. "It's a good thing Lucy didn't come," she whispered, looking at Polly sideways. "She'd have messed it all up. She's useless at dance. She doesn't have any sense of rhythm. And you're not much better."

Polly rolled her eyes. "At least she knows enough not to hang around with you any more."

Martha just smiled and shrugged, then wandered away, leaving Polly staring after her.

She knew that if she stirred Martha up she'd probably only be making things worse. But she just couldn't leave it. Somebody ought to teach Martha a lesson. Show her that she wasn't as special as she thought she was.

In the end Polly didn't even have to do anything. Martha was doing a particularly showy spin with Fran, one of the Year Five girls, and she ran into Polly's foot. Which just happened to be in her way because, as Martha had already pointed out, Polly didn't have a perfect sense of rhythm...

Martha tumbled down in a heap on the floor and glared at Polly. "You did that on purpose!"

Polly was too surprised to say anything but Miss Roberts shook her head. "No, she didn't. It was an accident. Are you both all right?"

"I think I've sprained my ankle," Martha whimpered, pulling herself up and wincing dramatically.

Polly leaned down to help her stand up. "I didn't do it on purpose," she whispered. "But you would have deserved it if I had."

"Oh! Polly, have you seen Lucy?"

Polly stopped at the door of the school, gazing in surprise at Lucy's gran.

"Lucy didn't come home after school and she hasn't called me. Her phone's turned off. I just wondered if you'd seen her."

Polly shook her head, stammering a little. "N-no … sorry. I went to dance club after school – it's only just finished. She didn't say that she was going anywhere."

"It must sound silly to be fretting about her," Lucy's gran murmured. "But she always, always calls since she got her phone and we let her walk back by herself. She promised and she always does…"

She had her hand on Polly's sleeve, holding on to it as though she couldn't bear to let her go. As though Polly was a thin, delicate thread to Lucy. "I came down to the school, I was so sure she must be here. Where else could she be?" She looked around helplessly, as if she expected to see Lucy appear at the other end of the corridor.

"Where would she go?" Polly asked worriedly.

"I don't know! She's been out an awful lot these last few days. She said she was just exploring by herself but I hoped maybe she'd gone home with you tonight. She had such a good time that afternoon she went to tea at yours."

"I did, too," Polly murmured. "But she only came that one day. Oh! I know somewhere she might go! Up on the cliff path – she showed me. A sort of den. Shall I go and look?"

"The path towards Penhallow? Would you? I should go back and check she hasn't come home. Thank you, Polly."

Polly set off on her usual way home, hurrying towards the cliff path. She got to the tangle of brambles around the old shed and was about to stop and call for Lucy when she noticed a flash of red just behind the tumbledown building. She stood on tiptoe, peering over the brambles, hoping to see Lucy. But the coloured fabric wasn't a school jumper. It was a bit of a tent, she realized slowly, and there were others a little further back, pitched on the narrow field between the road and the brambles. She could hear voices, too.

Lucy definitely wouldn't come here to hide out, not now there were people around. She'd really hoped that she would be able to help. Still, it was past five now. Surely Lucy would be home? Polly sighed and turned back for the village. It would be quicker to go home and call Lucy's house, but she was so worried now she wanted to see Lucy and make sure she was all right.

She hurried down the lane and shoved her way through the creaking wooden gate to the cottage. Lucy's gran met her at the door as though she'd been watching out of the window.

"She's not come back?" Polly asked, dismayed. She had been so sure that Lucy would be there.

Her gran looked somehow thinner and older than she had an hour before. "No… We've been taking it in turns to go out looking for her. I called her mum in the end, she's come back from work to help." She shook her head. "I thought about calling the police but I can't do that, not yet. I'm sure she'll be back soon…"

Polly nodded. "Yes. She'll be back." She tried
to sound certain but it was difficult. She stood
in front of Lucy's gran, clenching her fingers.
"Um. When she is, please could you ask her to
call me? To let me know she's OK?"

Lucy's gran smiled at her, and then leaned
over and gave her a hug. "Of course I will.
Bless you, love."

7

Searching for Lucy

"What is it?" Rex came bounding towards her as she walked along the cliff path for the second time, stopping to nuzzle at her anxiously. "Something's wrong. You took so long to come back home."

"No, no, it isn't me." Polly put her hands on either side of his face and stroked his muzzle lovingly. "Thank you for coming, Rex. I needed you. Lucy's gone. She disappeared after school and no one knows where she is."

Rex snorted worriedly. "That's not right…"

"Her gran's so worried. She says Lucy always

tells her where she's going." Polly looked over at the tents spread out on the other side of the brambles. "I was sure she'd be here but there's all those people." She sank down on to the ground with a tired sigh. "I don't know where to look."

She pulled up a handful of grass, throwing it across the path in frustration, and reached down for another one. But instead of grass, her hand met something hard, something that rattled as she picked it up. A key ring – a little dog, like the one Lucy had given her. The same, in fact. Lucy had bought herself another one to replace the one she'd given Polly.

Rex sniffed at her hand. "This belongs to her, doesn't it? She's been here, then. Today?"

Polly frowned. Had this been on Lucy's bag in school earlier? Yes, of course, because Lucy had shown it to her – she'd laughed and said the dogs were twins.

"Put it on the grass again." Rex sat down on the path next to her, his eyes closed and his ears laid back, resting one massive paw on the key ring. There were wrinkles around his muzzle and he almost looked as though he had a headache.

"What are you doing?" Polly whispered.

"Shh. I'm thinking. She's here, Polly. Not here on the clifftop but at Penhallow somewhere. I can feel her." He opened his eyes and looked up at Polly.

"Can you really tell that she's there? I didn't know you could do things like that."

"Not all the time, maybe." Rex heaved a huge sigh. "But she's on Penhallow ground, I'm sure of it. Worried. Hiding. I can definitely feel *that*. We have to find her, Polly. I can't bear it, now that I know she's there. We have to help her."

"So can you tell where she actually is?"

Rex made a snorting, huffing noise. "What do you think I am, some sort of bloodhound? No, I cannot. She's at Penhallow – somewhere in the house or the grounds. That's all I know."

Polly peered over the tops of the bramble bushes and along the path to where she could see the house in the distance.

"I suppose it's better than not knowing where she is at all." She sighed. "But I wish we had more to go on."

"We should wake Skip," Rex said suddenly, his tail starting to swing. "Yes! He had more of a connection with her than I did. He'll know where she is."

"But we can't," Polly pointed out. "He's in the nursery and it's still half an hour before closing time. There'll be people there."

Rex shook his ears irritably. "Then we'll just have to get rid of them. This is urgent, Polly. I can feel it."

Polly nodded and they set off at a jog back to the house.

"I'd better go and tell Mum I'm home," Polly said to Rex, as they dashed through the front door. "I can leave my stuff in her office, then I don't have to go all the way up to the flat."

Rex snorted in agreement, then turned away from her, half leaping up the main stairs, his great legs taking the steps three at a time.

Polly watched him for a moment, her mouth hanging open, and then darted down the passage to her mum's office.

"Are you all right? You look a bit frazzled…"

"Lucy disappeared after school, and her mum and her gran don't know where she is," Polly gabbled. "She really liked the house when she came here with me, so I'm just going to look around in case she's here. Is that OK?"

"Of course it is." Her mum looked worriedly at her. "Do you want some help? I can come and look, too."

Polly sighed. "Thanks, Mum. I don't even know that she's here, though. It's just – I don't want to do nothing."

"All right. I've got a couple of calls I have to make, then I'll come and help."

Polly nodded, then hurried off to chase after Rex. She found him at the end of the nursery passageway, his tail twitching as he gazed towards the nursery door.

"What are we going to do?" Polly whispered. "We can't just go and take him."

"Mmmm. No," Rex agreed. "But we could if everyone was out of the room, couldn't we?" Before Polly could grab his collar, he jumped up on to his hind legs and pushed heavily against an ugly china vase that was standing on a pedestal at the top of the stairs.

Polly was halfway through saying, "You can't do that!" when the vase hit the stairs with a thundering crash and went on to bounce down several steps in about thirty pieces.

"It was very ugly," Rex said ruthlessly. "Now, you'd better hide or they'll think you did it. I'll come back for you with Skip."

Polly ducked back round the corner of the passage and into one of the rooms that wasn't open to visitors. She stood half inside the door, hoping that no one would notice her. Rex stalked away from her up the passage, just as the visitors and staff from the nursery rooms came hurrying out to investigate the noise. He was back a few seconds later, with the saggy old dog clutched in his teeth.

"Come on," he mumbled. "Hurry up."

"Sorry! I just… I wasn't sure what you were going to do. I can't believe you broke that thing!"

"This is more important. Down the corridor." Rex galloped away, the toy dog swinging.

"We can't get back to the stairs, though!" Polly gasped, hurrying after him. "They're covered in bits of vase."

"Don't need to. In here." He scrabbled at a door and it swung open, revealing a tiny room painted a yellowy white and fitted with shelves and cupboards, all very dusty and rickety with age.

"I've never been in here." Polly looked around, curious in spite of herself.

"It's the old nursery kitchen. Not really a kitchen, though. There was a gas ring for cocoa, that's all. But this is what we need." He gestured with his head towards a large wooden panel in the wall and the toy dog swung from side to side again.

"Let me go," snarled a cross little voice, and the dog in Rex's jaws wriggled. "Stop waving me about and put me down!"

"Oh. Sorry." Rex set him on the floor and the white terrier glared at him. He looked so cross but one of his ears stood up straight and the other flopped over sideways. It made it hard to take him seriously.

"What do you mean by dragging me around like this? I told you to leave me alone."

"We're sorry," Polly broke in. "We didn't want to bother you but we need your help."

"Mine?" Skip looked disbelieving but both his ears lifted just a little, as if he were intrigued.

"Yes, do you remember the girl I brought to see you? The one with the blond wavy hair. She came to the nursery and she stroked you, and she said you were lovely. Do you remember?"

"Yes," the dog agreed cautiously. "What of it?"

"She's lost and we thought maybe you could help us find her?"

"Lost…" Skip flinched back, his skew-whiff ears flat against his skull and his tail disappearing so far between his legs that his back went rounded.

Polly looked at him wide-eyed. Obviously the word, the idea of being lost, terrified him. "We really want to find her," she said gently. "We want to take her home."

"Home…" The little dog only whispered it but Polly felt her eyes fill with tears.

"Yes," she murmured. "We thought you might be able to tell where she was."

The dog relaxed a little, standing straighter again. "I suppose I could look…"

"Please will you? Now?" Polly begged. "We're worried about her."

The white dog stepped towards the door but Rex leaned over to shoo him back.

"No, not that way. I, er … the stairs are out of bounds at the moment. We'll take the lift."

"The lift?" Polly blinked. "We can't, it's only for wheelchairs. And you can't get to it from here anyway, it doesn't come up to this floor."

"This lift goes all the way down to the kitchens," Rex told her patiently.

"Oh, the dumb waiter," Skip agreed. "I went in it with Jack once."

"The what?" Polly looked at them blankly.

"The dumb waiter. It's a little lift to bring food from the kitchens for nursery meals. You pull it up and down with a rope." Skip jumped up and clawed at the base of the panel so that it slid bumpily away and up into the wall, revealing a dark opening, hazed with cobwebs.

"You mean we're getting in that?" Polly asked, staring at it doubtfully.

The two dogs stared at her. "Well, I don't *need* to," Rex pointed out. "I could just sneak down the stairs. And so could Skip. But you can't, can you? And I thought you'd prefer it if we stayed."

Polly swallowed. "Yes. Yes, I would. All right. Is it safe?" She looked closer in and drew her finger across the dusty floor.

"Of course it is. It's perfectly reliable," Rex said soothingly. "In you get."

Polly climbed into the dumb waiter, crouching tightly in the small space, and shut her eyes as it rocked underneath her. "Where does it come out?" she hissed, as Skip jumped in and scrambled on to her lap, and Rex set his huge front paws on the edge so he could wriggle round behind her.

"In the old sculleries, don't worry. All closed
up, no visitors there. Now, where's that rope?
Ah. Here."

Polly squeaked as the dumb waiter lurched
underneath her. The floor seemed to drop away
and she felt her insides leap up into her throat

as the little wooden box plummeted down.

"Of course," she heard Rex say thoughtfully in the darkness, "it hasn't actually been used for a good many years..."

"How many?" she wailed, as they crashed down to the floor. But a cloud of dust billowed up around them and her words were lost in a storm of coughing.

8

The Shelter

Rex and Polly followed Skip as he darted around the gardens, sniffing and scrabbling.

"I can smell her," he kept muttering to himself, and then, "Ah! Over here!" and he would dash away again, desperate to follow the scent he'd picked up from Lucy's key ring.

"Hold still," Rex demanded at last, after they'd been all round the main gardens twice. "Can you track her or not? Stop racing back and forth like that and calm down."

Skip halted, trembling with eagerness. "I can

smell her," he said again. "I know she's here, somewhere… I just can't tell where." He shook himself all over and Polly saw that the whites were showing around his eyes. "It's like Annie," he muttered. "She was always wandering off. She was so little and everyone was too busy to watch her. I used to sniff her out… She was in the stables once. Another time it was one of the old kitchen cupboards – she was playing with the pans."

Polly looked at her watch – six o'clock already. Perhaps she should tell Lucy's mum or her gran that Lucy was at Penhallow. But how? The key ring wasn't really that much of a clue and she could hardly say that the dogs had told her.

Skip's ears suddenly pricked up – even his floppy ear stood up for half a second, and his whiskers seemed to quiver. "I know where she is!" he yelped. Then he whisked away, racing round the corner of the house.

"Where's he off to?" Rex panted, hurrying after the smaller dog. By the time they had reached the corner, Skip had disappeared, lost somewhere in the mass of outbuildings and stables that stood around the back of the house. Rex stood staring around and then heaved a huge sigh.

"There are too many scents around here to track him," he said. "We've all been running through the kitchen yard. I can't work out which scent is the freshest." He put his nose down to sniff again. "He must be somewhere close. We weren't that far behind – he must have disappeared into one of these doorways."

Polly looked around, frowning. "Rex, do you know where the air-raid shelter is? My mum mentioned that there was one and that it was close to the kitchens. Skip was talking about

Annie playing in a kitchen cupboard when he dashed off like that."

Rex eyed her doubtfully. "I don't see how Lucy would have found the air-raid shelter."

"I did tell her there were rooms that were never opened," Polly said, thinking it through. "There must be hundreds of places to hide here. If that's what she wants, I bet the shelter would be perfect. It has beds and everything."

"Mmmm. Maybe. I still don't see what she's hiding from!" Rex shook his ears crossly. "And I don't know where it is." He paced across the yard outside the scullery and sighed again.

"Mum said she thought it might be close to the kitchens," Polly put in.

Rex nodded. "If I were trying to make a safe place, I would have used the old wine cellars, I think. But most of them were blocked off years ago. Could we get to them from the kitchens, perhaps…?"

He eyed the back door to the scullery uncertainly and then he froze, staring towards a tiny barred window, mostly below floor level. A worn flight of little stone steps led down to a heavily bolted door. The glass behind the bars was half missing and floating out from the opening were the familiar notes of a song.

She knew it – it was 'We'll Meet Again', one of the songs they'd learned at school.

For a moment Polly's heart seemed to stop, then it raced to catch up, thumping hard. That was a wartime song. Who could be singing it? The sound was thin and strange – almost eerie – as it seeped up from the stonework. For a moment Polly was sure that ghosts were singing.

She drew closer to Rex, wanting the warmth and comfort of his fur. He might be not far off a ghost himself but he wasn't scary. She wrapped her arm round his neck, feeling the song catch her and carry her along.

Then she sighed and the fear drained away. *They had learned it at school.* "Lucy!" she whispered.

"No…" Rex shivered. "That's an old song, I can tell. Lots of memories caught up in there."

The hairs along his back were standing up in a ridge.

"It is her, Rex, I'm sure. We learned that song for our wartime topic."

Rex looked round at her. "You're truly sure?" He shook himself and his coat lay flat again. "Very well. Let's find her then. That's definitely part of the old cellars. We just have to work out how she got in."

He led Polly on a winding tour of the warren of Penhallow kitchens, carefully avoiding the parts that were dressed up to show to visitors – the old scullery where the great copper was for laundry, and the main kitchen with its range and scrubbed table, and the huge old pans and jelly moulds hanging from the walls. Instead they hurried through ghostly, empty rooms, Rex's claws clacking on the stone flags. There was no sign of an air-raid shelter – or Lucy.

"We've been through here already," Polly said, stopping to catch her breath as Rex went darting into another chill bare room. This one had a great stone chimney breast, dark with what looked like centuries of soot.

He looked back at her, the golden fur round his muzzle grey with dust. "Have we? Oh, yes… She must be here somewhere."

"Listen!" Polly wound her fingers in his fur, her heart thudding as she heard the song again.

"Is that coming down the chimney?" Rex paced forward, peering cautiously into the dark gap. "There must have been a stove in here once. Or an open fire."

"Look…" Polly nudged him, pointing towards a black iron door at the side of the fireplace. It had been hidden by the stonework until they looked right in.

"A secret cellar?" Rex nosed at the door and it

swung open a little further.

Polly shuddered as a gust of colder air rolled around their feet. "There are stairs leading down," she whispered to Rex. "This has to be it, doesn't it?"

"Yes! Look!" Rex nodded towards a dusty patch in front of the iron door and she saw that there were footprints – footprints and pawprints in the dust.

"I know this is what we're looking for," Polly said, "but I really don't like it."

"Hold on to my collar." Rex pressed his damp black nose against her cheek and they began to creep down the flight of steps. Polly gripped tightly on to Rex's collar until they emerged into a dingy room fitted with beds all around the walls.

Staring back at her from a bed against the far wall was Lucy – and clutched in her lap was a small white dog.

Polly opened her mouth to say, "You found her!" to Skip, but then she realized that this was a dog that Lucy could quite clearly see and feel. She had her arm round him and he was snuggled against her. He wasn't quite the same shape as Skip, either. His legs were a little shorter and his muzzle was longer. But Polly knew who he was.

"That's the stray dog that Stephen told me
to look out for… You found him." Polly's eyes
widened. "You found him days ago, didn't you?"

Polly sat down next to Lucy on the bed,
feeling as though her knees had given way.
"And the day you came and had tea with us,
that was why you were on the path! Were you
keeping him in that stone shed? I thought that
whining noise was you crying but it was the
dog all along! I even saw him, when we walked

back to yours. He was in the window, watching after us."

"Sorry," Lucy whispered. "He's such a sweet dog and … and I wanted to look after him. I went out looking for him, after you told me, and it was as if he was waiting for me to find him. He was in the lane just sitting there and he let me stroke him, and then he disappeared under the hedge. But then he was back the next morning before school and he came with me after I fed him. I gave him most of my packed lunch."

Polly nodded slowly. She edged slowly closer and looked sideways at the little dog, trying not to scare him. She put her hand next to him on the bed so he could choose to sniff it if he wanted to.

The little white dog leaned over, sniffed her carefully and then licked her once before curling himself back up on Lucy's lap.

"Did Gran send you to look for me?" Lucy asked, staring down at the dog.

"Not exactly. She was at school and she told me you'd disappeared. I thought you might be on the cliff path again and I found your key ring. Then I thought maybe you'd come here. I'd told you about all those empty rooms… I was looking around and I heard you singing…"

"I was singing to him," Lucy explained. "He was a bit jumpy. I had to move him from the shed, you see. There were people camping up on the cliff when I went up there after school. People camp there in the summer, sometimes, but I never thought there'd be anyone up there now and I didn't want them to find him. So I thought there had to be somewhere around here we could hide out for a bit. I was going to come home soon. Sorry…" she added, looking at Polly worriedly. "I'll find somewhere else to keep him. I don't want to get you into trouble."

"How did you get in?" Polly asked.

"Just sneaked through the gardens – he seemed to know where he was going. He was hanging around here before I saw him in the village, wasn't he?"

Polly nodded. "I suppose so."

The white dog looked up at Polly and yawned. He was most definitely a real, solid dog. But they had been following Skip… Polly eyed the white dog and then looked round at Rex, trying not to be too obvious about it.

"You're such a lovely boy," Lucy murmured, and the white dog gazed up at her, pricking up his ears to listen. Then one of his ears flopped over again and Lucy laughed. "I love it when his ears do that."

"Yes," Polly whispered.

"That's Skip," Rex murmured. He sounded fascinated. "It is and it isn't. What's he done?"

"He's real," Polly said, and then she realized that she'd said it out loud.

Lucy giggled. "Of course he is. But I know what you mean. The way he kept appearing and disappearing, it was almost like I imagined him." She smiled at Polly.

"Couldn't you tell your mum about him? And your gran? Don't they like dogs?"

Lucy sighed. "I suppose I'll have to – I can't keep hiding him forever. Especially not when it gets colder. But I'm just worried they'll say no and then what would I do?" She scratched the dog behind his ears. "Gran loves dogs and I think Mum does, too. It's just Dad who wasn't keen on having one. If I promised to do all the looking after, maybe they'd let me keep him?"

"It sounds like they might." Polly nodded.

"They must," Rex whispered beside her. "This is meant to happen. You should tell her to take the dog home."

"I really am sorry," Lucy murmured. "For making you look for me and everything."

"It's OK. Weird stuff's happened to me, too. Oh!" She giggled. "I tripped up Martha."

"What?" Lucy stared at her.

"At dancing. She was being mean again and then somehow she fell over me." Polly smiled, remembering. "It was *perfect*." Then she added hurriedly, "It's OK, she wasn't actually hurt. And I didn't really do it on purpose." She paused for a second. "Even though I wish I had."

Lucy laughed. "Thanks." She bent down to kiss the top of the white dog's head and he buried his black nose in the crook of her neck.

"He's turned real because she needed him," Polly whispered to Rex.

"I think so," Rex agreed, leaning in to look at the smaller dog. "It was the magic. My magic," he added rather loftily, but then Skip leaned over to sniff at him and licked his nose, making Rex stumble back.

"Well, he seems quite happy," he muttered.

Polly nodded at him and then checked her watch. "We should get you home," she said gently. "Your gran's really worried. And she called your mum. I'd take the dog back with you, too – then you can explain why you disappeared."

"Yes, I suppose so." Lucy made a face and stood up. "All right. Come on, little one."

"What are you going to call him?" Polly asked, and Lucy stopped, looking down in surprise.

"Oh! I hadn't thought." She frowned. "Do you think Skip's a good name? He just … looks like a Skip."

"It suits him." Polly looked over her shoulder to smile at Rex and then her smile faded.

Rex hadn't noticed her. He was looking back at the bed where they'd been sitting, his tail beating slowly from side to side. He was staring at two children, sitting close to each other on the bed. A boy and a girl, younger than Polly and Lucy, in the same strange, old-fashioned clothes they'd been wearing in the school photograph.

They were smiling at Rex and as Polly watched, they saw her, too. Annie clutched her toy dog tighter and then lifted her hand to wave.

"Look after him," Jack said huskily.

Polly swallowed and nodded, and a thread of music floated across the room as the children faded into nothing.

Polly laid her hand on Rex's neck and he turned to nose at her, burying his great head in her arms. "I think they're happier now," she whispered. "All three of them."

Toy dog
left behind
January 1940

HOLLY WEBB
The HOUNDS of PENHALLOW HALL
THE MOONLIGHT STATUE
Illustrated by
JASON COCKCROFT

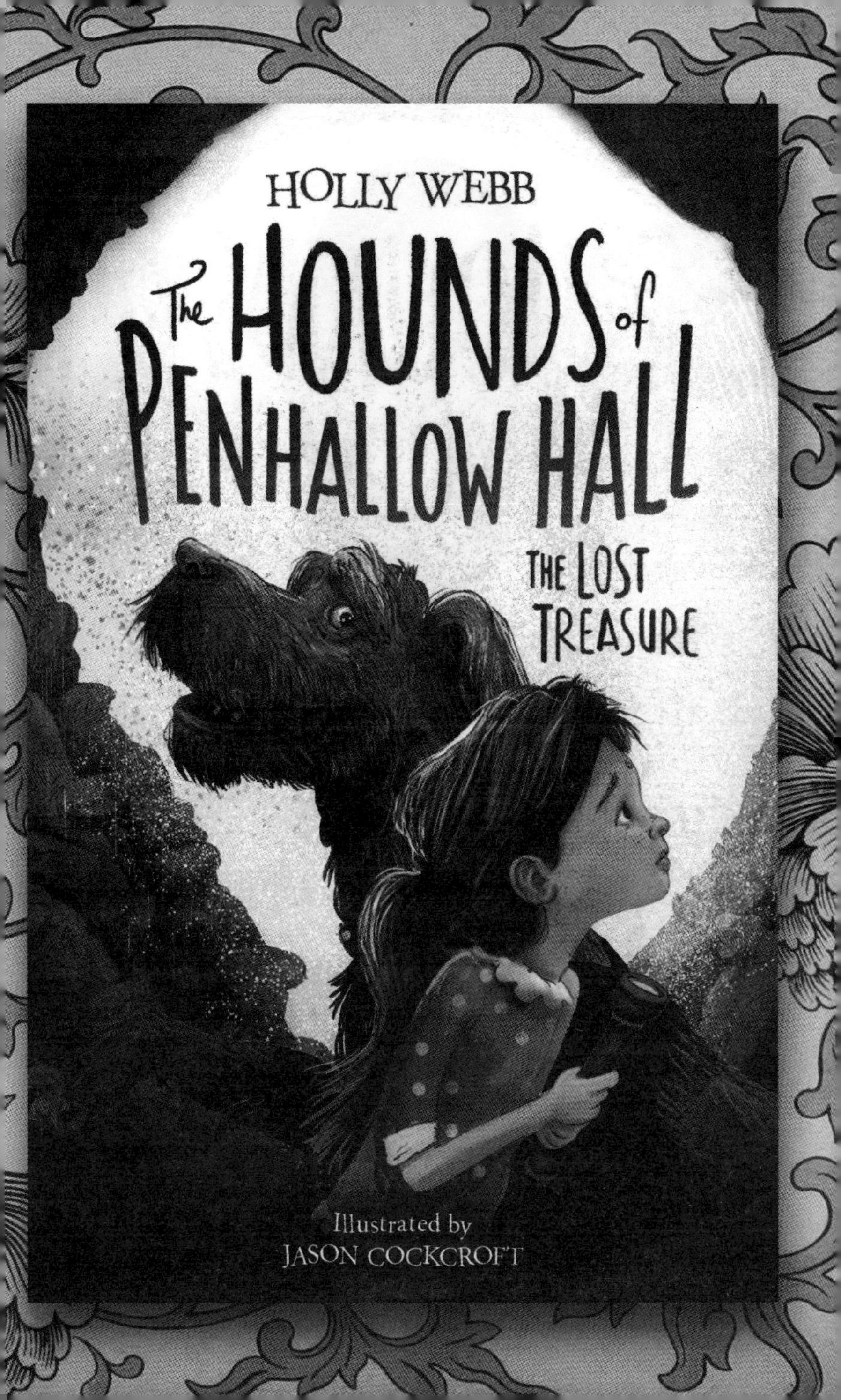
HOLLY WEBB
The HOUNDS of PENHALLOW HALL
THE LOST TREASURE
Illustrated by
JASON COCKCROFT

Holly Webb started out as a children's book editor and wrote her first series for the publisher she worked for. She has been writing ever since, with over one hundred books to her name. Holly lives in Berkshire, with her husband and three young sons. Holly's pet cats are always nosying around when she is trying to type on her laptop.

~

For more information about Holly Webb visit www.holly-webb.com